THE ORIENT EXPRESS

AN EROTIC ADVENTURE

VICTORIA RUSH

VOLUME 31

JADE'S EROTIC ADVENTURES - BOOK 31

COPYRIGHT

The Orient Express © 2020 Victoria Rush

Cover Design © 2020 PhotoMaras

FEEL THE RUSH:

Jade's Erotic Adventures – Book 1

When lonely divorcée Jade seeks to broaden her horizons, she's invited to a private dinner event which promises to stimulate all of her senses. Wearing nothing but masquerade masks, dinner guests receive special service under the table while their fellow diners look on...

The Dinner Party

Jade's Erotic Adventures - Book 2

Jade discovers an exotic adventure club where strangers meet to explore each other's bodies in mysterious dark rooms. Using special effects to project swirling light patterns onto their figures, the shifting shadows provide just enough illumination to highlight their naked bodies while protecting their identities...

The Dark Room

Jade's Erotic Adventures - Book 3

Jade discovers a yoga club where members stretch and explore each other's bodies in the buff. She books an appointment, and during the first session meets a young redhead who tantalizes her with her flexibility and stunning body...

Naked Yoga

For the uninhibited...

As I rubbed my thighs together thinking of the way she'd touched me earlier, Adele suddenly passed by me and took a seat four booths down, sitting on the edge of the aisle, facing toward me. At first, I was disappointed that she hadn't decided to join me in my section, and I wondered if she just hadn't noticed me with my back turned away from her. But when she peered up at me and smiled, I nodded to acknowledge her reaction. I didn't want to intrude on her personal space, but what she did next left little doubt that she was far from being done with me. She lifted her left leg and placed her foot on top of the seat cushion next to her and hiked up her dress a few inches, revealing her bare, glistening pussy. Then she placed her hand between her thighs and began circling her fingers over the top of her slit.

I looked around me to see if anyone else could see what she was doing, but fortunately all the other guests were sitting snugly against their windows, either reading a book or quietly gazing outside. Because we were the only two people in the compartment sitting on the outside edges of our booths, we had a direct view of each other. At first, I sat dumbfounded watching her play with herself, shocked at her audacious display of carnality, but as my panties grew wetter and wetter watching her, I looked around me to make sure the coast was clear, then I lifted my ass off my seat and pulled my panties down over my ankles and placed them inside my purse. Then I pushed my hand under my dress and slid my fingers up my thighs until they reached my sopping sex.

When they touched my burning clit, I gasped from how turned on I was, and Adele smiled at me from the other end of the cabin. I didn't have the courage to hike up my dress the way she had for fear that a passing porter or passenger might catch me in the act, but it certainly didn't stop me from fingering myself furiously while I watched the sexy French woman touching herself. Adele spread her legs further apart, exposing her bald, glistening snatch, then she thrust two fingers deep into her hole as she began finger-fucking herself with her flexing arm muscles...

1
____

E ntering the Gare du Nord terminal in Paris, I peered up at the soaring glass ceiling enclosing the cavernous central hall. Knowing it was the busiest train station in Europe, I held my arms close to my sides to protect my valuables from ever-present pickpockets. Designed by the famous French architect Jacques Hittorff in the Beaux-Arts style of the mid-nineteenth century, I marveled at the ornate cast-iron pillars supporting the enormous structure. It was a clear sunny day, and bright beams of light angled through the windows, illuminating the shiny trains resting beside their platforms. I glanced at my ticket and headed toward gate eighteen, where I was about to embark on a five-day/four-night tour of Europe aboard the most famous train in history.

Passing through the pastoral countryside of southern France and the deep valleys of the Swiss Alps, the Orient Express wound its way through seven countries, terminating at the gateway to Asia in Istanbul. With its storied past and recently refurbished equipment, I was looking forward to being pampered in the five-star dining car and my own private cabin on the traveling caravan. I'd heard so much about the glamor and prestige of the famous line, and as I approached the black-and-gold vintage train cars sitting by the platform, my heart began to flutter in excitement.

Near the front of the train, a porter wearing a brass-buttoned uniform and white gloves checked my ticket then helped me up the steps into the forward compartment. When I stepped into the carriage, I was shocked at how opulent it looked. The main salon was decorated with sumptuous velour upholstery, polished cherry wood paneling, crystal lanterns, and giant windows framed with royal blue curtains. More beautiful than any luxury hotel I'd ever stayed in, the setting literally took my breath away.

"Oh my God," I muttered to the porter. "It's like I've entered a whole different world. This isn't like any train I've been on before."

"That's a common reaction from our first-time travelers," he said. "Our owners have spared no expense in recreating the feel and authenticity of the original train. If you like the main seating area, I think you'll be very pleased with your cabin. I see you've chosen the grand suite."

"Yes," I nodded. "I figured if I'm going to splurge on a luxury train ride, I might as well go all the way."

"I think you'll find the extra space is quite comfortable. You've got three large viewing windows, your own sitting area, and a large private washroom."

"Well if it's anything like the rest of the train," I said, tracing my fingers along the luxurious upholstery as we passed by the four-person seating booths, "I'm sure I'll be delighted."

We walked through two more carriages down a narrow passageway then he stopped by a polished wooden door with a brass handle.

"Here we are, madam," he said, opening the door and motioning for me to enter ahead of him with his gloved hand.

I stepped into the anteroom and gasped out loud. The entire chamber gleamed in a mixture of knurled walnut paneling, crystal light fixtures, and suede seat coverings. The king-size bed was festooned with plush Egyptian-cotton linens and blue-and-gold embroidered cushions, with outside light streaming in the huge viewing windows lining the entire side of the compartment."

"It's...*breathtaking*," I said, hardly believing my eyes. "It's the most beautifully bedroom I've ever seen. Is this all just for *me*?"

"Yes, ma'am," the porter said, opening another door next to the sitting area. "As is this private ensuite bathroom."

I peered inside the washroom, my eyes opening as wide as saucers.

Almost every surface was covered in polished alabaster marble. From the large, glass-enclosed walk-in shower to the brass taps on the vanity to the separately enclosed toilet, everything reeked of first class. It even had a separate, sit-down makeup table, replete with Lalique crystal lamps.

"If I ever get to heaven," I sighed. "This is what I hope it looks like."

"I'm glad you like it, ma'am," the porter said. "As part of your grand suite package, you also have twenty-four-hour butler service, private in-cabin dining, and free-flowing champagne for the duration of your trip."

"Okay, so *wait*," I chuckled. "Are you sure I'm not *already* in heaven?"

The porter set my bags down on the floor and backed up toward the entrance door.

"Please, make yourself comfortable," he said. "If you need

anything at all, press this button and your butler will call upon you shortly. Dinner in the main cabin will be served starting at seven p.m. But the bar is open twenty-four-seven. I hope you enjoy your stay with us."

"I only wish it could be longer," I smiled, discreetly handing him a ten-Euro tip. "Are you sure this train doesn't go any further than Istanbul?"

"For now, at least," he said. "That's the end of the line. But I've heard rumors our operator is considering extending the service into the Middle East and beyond, following the path of the Silk Road used by Marco Polo."

"Now that would be a truly memorable journey," I nodded. "It *is* called the Orient Express, after all."

After the porter left, I unpacked my bags and changed into something more befitting the glamorous setting, then I went into the washroom to touch up my makeup. When I finished, I looked at myself in the full-length dressing mirror and nodded in satisfaction. I'd chosen to wear a form-fitting, mid-length red silk dress with black leather Christian Louboutin heels that showcased my long, well-toned legs. As the train began to pull out of the station, I pulled the door to my cabin closed behind me and headed toward the bar car.

Let's see if the guests on this caravan are as interesting as the rest of the train, I smiled.

When I reached the bar car, I noticed a scattering of passengers chatting in the plush velour booths beside the window. I peered up toward the bar and saw an elegant woman sitting alone on one of the stools with her back toward me. She was wearing a cream-colored lace embroidered dress, and I glanced down to see her slender and shapely legs crossed under the brass railing. I walked up to the counter and smiled at the bartender.

"Good evening, madam," he said. "Would you like something to drink?"

"Yes, thank you," I said, looking at the row of liquor bottles lining the wall behind him. I was about to order a Grey Goose martini when I noticed the woman was cradling a tall tulip glass filled with a pale yellow mixture with bubbles rising to the surface. "I think I'll have what the lady's having."

"Dom Perignon it *is*," he nodded. He pulled a magnum off the shelf and carefully loosened the cork to let out the air before tilting the bottle over a carved crystal glass and sliding it toward me.

"May I join you?" I said, glancing at the lady sitting next to me.

"By all means," she smiled, uncrossing her legs and lifting her knee over her opposite leg.

As I sat down and turned my stool to face her, I noticed for the first time her plunging neckline and deep cleavage pressing her plump breasts together. She had long auburn-colored hair, styled with curly ringlets framing her pretty face. She looked to be around my age, but with slightly darker skin. She had a vaguely European look to her, and as she peered at me with her smoldering eyes, I felt my panties beginning to moisten.

"Cheers," I said, holding up my glass.

"Santé," she replied, clinking her champagne flute against mine.

"This is quite the experience, isn't it?" I said, looking around me at the ornately decorated cabin.

"Is this your first time?" she said with a French accent.

"Aboard the Orient Express? Yes. How about you?"

"This is my third trip. I find the experience to be quite stimulating."

"Are you referring to the amazing views?" I said, peering outside the window behind her at the passing Paris streetscape.

"That, and you meet the most interesting people on this voyage," she nodded. "We're all captive on this little train while we're traveling, and you get to know everybody pretty well."

"I can imagine," I said, flittering my eyes downward to take in her voluptuous figure. Her nipples were pressing hard against the sheer lacy fabric, and I crossed my legs, feeling my pussy growing wetter by the moment.

"Where are you from?" she said, peering down at my exposed thighs as she took another sip of her champagne. "You don't have a British, Aussie, or Kiwi accent, so I'm guessing you're either American or Canadian."

"I'm from Chicago," I said, chuckling at her deductive powers. "How about you?"

"I'm from the Alsace region of France, near the German border."

"I thought I recognized some Continental genes in your appearance. You're very pretty."

"As are you," she said, placing her hand on my knee and sliding it softly up my thigh. "You American girls always take such good care of your bodies. I like how you're so toned and fit. We Europeans take a much more laissez-faire approach to our fitness."

"Thank you," I said, feeling the soft hairs on the top of my thighs standing erect as her hand caressed my skin. Suddenly I wished I'd remembered to shave the full length of my legs more recently.

"I'm Jade, by the way," I said, extending my hand to distract attention from the other passengers glancing at us nearby.

"Adele," she said, clasping my hand and squeezing it gently. Even the touch of her hand against mine sent a chill through my spine.

"So, what do people do to pass their time for five straight days on this little chugger?" I asked, trying to regain my composure.

"Besides eating and drinking most of the time?" she chuckled. "Most people curl up with a book next to the window to watch the passing scenery. But at meal time, everybody gets together in the dining car, where we can mingle a bit more comfortably."

"Speaking of drinking," I said, realizing the bartender had already replenished my glass three times while I'd been talking. "I'm already starting to feel a bit tipsy. If I don't get off this bar stool soon, I'm afraid I'll fall over. I think curling up in one of those comfortable booths by the window is just what I need about now. Would you care to join me?"

"Perhaps a little later," she said, rising up from her stool. "Right now I need to make a trip to the ladies' room. But I look forward to meeting you again soon, lovely Jade."

While I watched her head down the hall toward the public lavatory, I couldn't help staring at her tight ass in her form-fitting dress as her buttocks flexed sexily under the sheer lacy fabric. I staggered to the nearest seat a few feet from the bar and rested my head against the backrest as I peered out over the passing landscape of the French countryside. I felt surprisingly lightheaded for only having had three drinks. Whether it was from drinking on an empty stomach or from the passing vineyards rushing by my window or from the excitement of meeting this mysterious and sexy woman, I couldn't be sure. Either way, my trip aboard the Orient Express had gotten off to an exciting start.

As I rubbed my thighs together thinking of the way she'd touched me, Adele suddenly passed by me and took a seat four booths down, sitting on the edge of the aisle, facing toward me. At first, I was disappointed that she hadn't decided to join me in my section, and I wondered if she just hadn't noticed me with my back turned away from her. But when she peered up at me and smiled, I nodded to acknowledge her reaction. I didn't want to intrude on her personal space, but what she did next left little doubt that she was far from being done with me. She lifted her left leg and placed her foot on top of the seat cushion next to her and hiked up her dress a few inches, revealing her bare, glistening pussy. Then she placed her hand between her thighs and began circling her fingers over the top of her slit.

I looked around me to see if anyone else could see what she was doing, but fortunately all the other guests were sitting snugly against their windows, either reading a book or quietly gazing outside. Because we were the only two people in the compartment sitting on the outside edges of our booths, we had a direct view of each other. At first, I sat dumbfounded watching her play with herself, shocked at her audacious display of carnality, but as my panties grew wetter and wetter watching her, I looked around me to make sure the coast was clear, then I lifted my ass off my seat and pulled my panties down over my ankles and placed them inside my purse. Then I pushed my hand under my dress and slid my fingers up my thighs until they reached my sopping sex.

When they touched my burning clit, I gasped from how turned on I was, and Adele smiled at me from the other end of the cabin. I didn't have the courage to hike up my dress the way she had for fear that a passing porter or passenger might catch me in the act, but it certainly didn't stop me from fingering myself furiously while I watched the sexy French woman touching herself. Adele spread her legs further apart, exposing her bald, glistening snatch, then she thrust two fingers deep into her hole as she began finger-fucking herself with her flexing arm muscles.

I could hear the rumbling of the train as it passed speedily over the tracks, and the imagery of our pleasing ourselves in this strange but exciting public place elevated my passion even higher. As I felt my pleasure beginning to radiate throughout my body, I couldn't help squirming in my seat and pinching my nipples with my free hand. Apparently, Adele was equally turned on by the erotic scene, with her mouth beginning to part from her own rising pleasure while she stared back at me from across the aisle.

I could tell that she was nearing the crest of her pleasure as her face began to flush and her hand began moving more vigorously in and out of her dripping pussy. I began to feel my own orgasm rapidly approaching, and I pressed my hand harder up against my burning clit, unaware that my own dress was now hiked up near the top of my thighs, exposing my own bald and glistening vulva. Suddenly, a deep flush rolled over both of our faces as we began jerking spastically in our seats with our bodies consumed in a powerful simultaneous orgasm. We didn't take our eyes off each other the whole time while we gazed at one another with our mouths wide agape.

It must have taken a full thirty seconds for my contractions to subside, and when my orgasm finally receded, I slumped in my seat with my legs still spread wide apart. It was only then that I noticed in horror that someone *else* had been watching us the whole time. Just a few feet behind

Adele in the next compartment sat a young teenage girl peering through the crack in the seats with wide eyes, staring directly toward me. I closed my legs immediately and pulled my dress down over my thighs, then squiggled over closer to the window, shocked and humiliated. As I looked out the glass with my heart beating a million miles an hour, I felt my juices slowly trickling out of my wet pussy while I reflected on the exciting moment Adele and I had shared in the open compartment of the famed transcontinental express.

2

After I'd had a chance to calm down, I rested my head against my seat cushion and peered out over the passing landscape. The neatly spaced rows of vineyards provided a hypnotic counterpoint to the stimulating view of Adele playing with herself across the cabin, and before long I felt my eyelids grow heavy as I began to nod off. But just before I was about to pass out, I caught some movement from Adele's end of the carriage. The girl who'd been spying on us suddenly stood up and began side-stepping her way out of her cubicle.

She looked to be of middle eastern origin, with caramel-colored skin and large brown doe eyes. Her hair was pulled back into a ponytail, and with her high cheekbones and puffy lips, I was immediately struck by how beautiful she was. She could have easily passed for a young fashion model, but when she stepped out into the aisle, I gasped. Wearing a mid-length plaid skirt and matching green blazer with bow tie, it was obvious that she was just a schoolgirl. I couldn't make out how old she was, but from the shape of her body barely concealed by the short skirt and her bulging white blouse under her blazer, she certainly looked all grown up to me.

When she caught me staring at her, she winked at me playfully, then turned away and began walking toward the opposite end of the compartment. She hesitated for a moment outside the door to the public lavatory, then hiked up one side of her skirt, revealing an exquisitely toned and completely bare ass. Before entering the restroom, she glanced back at me and tilted her head, beckoning for me to follow her.

What the fuck? I thought to myself, shaking my head at my incredible streak of luck. *Was everybody on this train over-sexed and ready to jump on top of anyone they happened to bump into?*

I paused for a moment, contemplating my predicament. I didn't even know if the girl was of legal age to have sex. I took a closer look at her booth and saw a middle-aged man wearing a neatly pressed suit sitting close to the aisle. He had her same dark complexion and was reading a newspaper, seemingly oblivious to the sexually charged energy in the room. It seemed obvious to me that he was the girl's father or guardian, and I suspected he wouldn't look kindly upon my taking advantage of his daughter's youthful ardor.

But why was she dressed so provocatively, and why did she want me to join her in the lavatory? Had anyone *else* in the compartment noticed her libidinous display and was watching to see if I would join her? I glanced around the cabin and noticed that everyone was either staring outside their windows or had their heads bowed down tapping on their phones or laptop computers. If I was going to do something, I'd have to act soon before her father became suspicious of her extended absence.

Feeling the moisture beginning to accumulate once

again between my thighs, I raised myself out of my seat and began walking in the direction of the lavatory. When I passed Adele's booth, she peered up at me and smiled. With her body facing away from the direction of the girl's booth immediately behind her, I had no idea if she was aware of the special connection I'd made with the other passenger. But from the look of her swelling nipples in her form-fitting dress, she still appeared to be charged up from our earlier encounter.

As I passed by the girl's cubicle, her father glanced up from his newspaper and we nodded politely toward each other. Not wanting him to catch onto my lascivious intent, when I reached the closed door of the lavatory, I ducked into the adjacent cubbyhole near the train's exit door and leaned against the side wall with my heart pounding in my chest.

Holy shit! I cursed under my breath. *Was I really contemplating going through with this? What if we were found out? What if someone else needed to use the washroom while we were both inside?* It would be impossible to extricate ourselves without the other person knowing what we were up to in there. What if her *father* needed to use the washroom while we were busy making love to each other inside?

For a moment, I contemplated returning to my seat and dispensing with the whole idea. But the streams of lubrication running down the inside of my thighs was giving me second thoughts. When would I ever have a chance like this again? It's not every day that you get propositioned by a comely young schoolgirl to have a secret tryst with her on board the most famous train in the world.

Fuck it, I hissed, stepping forward to the lavatory door and tapping on it gently. Seconds later, the door opened a few inches and the girl peered out at me. I hesitated, not knowing what to say, then she reached out and pulled me inside, locking the door behind us. I looked at her with wide eyes, wondering what I had gotten myself into.

"Are you sure you want to do this?" I mumbled. "What about your father? How old are–"

The girl suddenly pulled me toward her, thrusting her tongue into my mouth while she pressed her hips and breasts against mine. When I felt her warm body against me and her tongue sliding over my teeth, everything else melted away as my hands began roaming over her curvy body. She tried to hike up my dress over my hips and press her hand between my legs, but I knew we didn't much time for the usual foreplay. I placed my hands under her armpits and lifted her ass up onto the edge of the sink, pressing her torso against the mirror. Then I lifted her plaid skirt and buried my face in her moist pussy.

At this point I no longer cared if she was of legal age. I intended to give her the best head she'd ever had, if indeed she'd ever had oral sex of *any* kind before. She had a narrow patch of pubic hair on her otherwise hairless mound, and as I sucked her swollen clit into my mouth, she placed her heels on top of the vanity and pulled my head hard into her cunt as she began squirming and moaning in delight. I was tempted to lift my hand to her mouth to muffle her squeals, but I figured the clattering of the train's metal wheels on the tracks was sufficient to drown out our mutual sounds of ecstasy.

Instead, I reached up and began unbuttoning her blouse, threading my hand inside her placket and squeezing her firm tits. I was surprised how large they were for a girl her age, and as her gushing juices began to coat the front of my face while I ate her out, I hooked my thumbs under the bottom of her bra and forced it up over top of her bosom. When I felt her bare melons filling my hands, I moaned along with her in rising pleasure. My own clit was throbbing between my outspread legs in my squatted position, and I would have loved to have ground it against her tender pussy, but I knew it would be difficult in the tight confines of the train lavatory to find enough room to properly scissor our bodies together.

Besides, I was enjoying eating the young girl's pussy and listening to her squeals of pleasure as I ravished her dripping cunny like it was my last meal. As she squirmed wildly on the edge of the counter, she placed her hands over the back of my head and began to dig her nails into my scalp. It was becoming apparent to me that she was nearing the crest of her pleasure, and as her squeals turned to impassioned whimpering, I placed her teats between my thumbs and forefingers and pinched her nipples firmly as she dug her nails ever-harder into my flesh.

Just when I thought I wouldn't be able to stand the pain any longer, her body suddenly lurched and she humped forward, jerking spastically over my head while she uttered a deep guttural moan. I held her close as I felt her juices pouring out of her hole and down over the front of my chin until she stopped heaving overtop of me. When she finally stopped moving, I pulled my face away from her pussy and she pushed herself off the edge of the counter and turned toward the mirror to pull her bra back in place and button herself back up. Then she turned around and glanced at me, reaching for the lock on the door.

"Thank you," she said with a faint Arabic accent, then she opened the door a crack and peered outside to make sure the coast was clear.

"*Wait*," I said, grasping her hand. "Can I see you again?"

"I better return to my seat before my father gets suspicious. Maybe if you can find a way to pass me your room number..."

I smiled at the girl and squeezed her hand as she left the compartment, then I closed and latched the door behind her. I'd never felt such a thrill in all my life, and I had matters of my own that needed attending to. Whether it was the possibility of having had sex with an underage girl, or the fact that we'd done it only a few feet away from her waiting father or the sheer audacity of having sex with a stranger in the train's public lavatory, I still felt incredibly turned on. As I hiked my dress up over my knees and plunged my hand between my legs, trilling my clit furiously while I bent over the stainless steel sink, I began to plot how I might entice the girl into a more comfortable setting to properly make love to her.

3

———

After cumming hard bent over the sink reliving my exciting liaison with the pretty schoolgirl, I returned to my seat in the main cabin and fell asleep with my head resting against the window. I awoke two hours later with a rumbling stomach, and noticing that the bar car had almost emptied out, I approached the bartender asking where I could get a bite to eat.

"Excuse me, sir," I said. "Which way is it to the dining car?"

"We have *two*, madam," he said. "The Cote D'Azur is the next car toward the front of the train, and the Hagia Sophia is the adjacent car to the rear."

"What's the difference?" I asked, wondering why in the world they would need two dining cars.

"The Cote D'Azur provides a continental menu, whereas the Hagia Sophia offers middle eastern fare."

"Wow, okay," I said, shaking my head at the continuing opulent array of choices on the luxury line.

I hesitated for a moment, then turned toward the aft section of the train, hoping to see another glimpse of the mysterious Arab girl. When I entered the adjoining carriage, my eyes widened at the sight that greeted me. The dining tables were immaculately set with neatly pressed white linen tablecloths, fine china, crystal drinking glasses, and sumptuous red velvet chairs. Most of the chairs were already occupied, but towards the rear of the compartment I noticed Adele sitting with the Arabian father and daughter pair, and I approached the table, motioning to the open seat.

"Do you have room for one more?" I asked, peering toward the gentleman.

"Of course," he said, rising politely and motioning for me to take the available seat.

I smiled toward the girl seated next to him at the window and nodded at Adele sitting next to me.

"I'm Jade," I said, extending my hand toward the gentleman.

"Omar," the man said. "And this is my daughter, Leila.

"And this lovely lady–" he said, motioning toward Adele.

"*Adele*–yes," I blushed. "We met earlier in the bar car."

"Perfect," he said, smiling toward his daughter. "I guess I'm the lucky one who'll be enjoying the company of three charming women over dinner this evening."

"Is this your first trip aboard the Orient Express?" I said, trying to break the awkward sexual tension at the table.

"Oh no," he said. "I make this trip often to visit my daughter in Paris. She's studying at the École Internationale."

"Oh?" I said, eager to hear more details about the mysterious girl. "What grade?"

"Lycée troisième," the girl said in a perfect French accent.

"My French is a little rusty," I smiled. "I'm not quite sure how that equates to our American education system."

"It's equivalent to grade 12 in the United States," Adele clarified.

"So you're a *senior* then," I nodded. "That would put you around seventeen–"

"I just turned eighteen," Leila replied matter-of-factly.

"You must be looking forward to graduating," I said, relieved to hear that she'd reached the age of majority. "I understand the Ecole Internationale is one of Europe's most exclusive private schools. Have you thought about where you'd like to go to college?"

"I've been accepted to Cambridge, La Sorbonne, and Harvard. But I'm leaning toward Harvard. I've never been to the United States–"

"I'd be happy to show you around if you'd like to visit. I have friends in the Boston area who I'm sure would be happy to put you up while you tour the campus."

"Really?" Leila said, her eyes perking up. "Where do you live in the States?"

"I'm from Chicago, but I do business in New England quite often. If you let me know when you'd like to come, I'm sure I could work my schedule around to accommodate you."

"That's very generous of you, Jade," Omar said, noticing the waiter approaching our table. "But we can talk about these matters later. Who's ready for something to eat?"

"I'm so hungry I could eat a horse, as we say in America," I said, winking at Leila.

"Well I don't know about *that*," Omar chuckled. "But I believe they serve lamb and Moroccan chicken if you prefer Arabian dishes."

"I'm definitely ready to sample more of your local fare," I smiled, feeling Leila tapping the outside of my foot under the table.

After we all ordered our meals, Adele excused herself to freshen up in the lavatory, and I took the opportunity to move over to the seat next to the window so I could be closer to Leila. When Adele returned, we talked about our travel plans and vocations. Omar ran an import-export business out of Istanbul and Adele was a finance executive with Commerzbank. The two of them struck up a conversation about foreign exchange rates, and before long Omar agreed to open an account at her bank. He then offered to let us stay at his villa on the Black Sea while we were in Turkey, to which both Adele and I readily agreed. Whether we were just happy to find any excuse to stay together during our layover or we were equally smitten by his beguiling daughter, was unclear. Either way, I was in no hurry to break up our happy little coterie.

When our meal service started with a shared plate of freshly baked pita and hummus, I noticed that Leila was growing increasingly frisky playing footsies with me under the table. By the time our main courses arrived, she'd already kicked off her shoes and was caressing the inside of my calves with her bare foot. Growing more emboldened by her father's seeming distraction with Adele's sexy lace dress and her continued efforts to solicit his banking business, she forced my knees apart and slowly began pressing her foot further up under my dress toward my bare crotch. When the ball of her foot began rubbing against my slippery vulva and twitching clit, I had a hard time concentrating on eating my meal. After a few minutes, Omar peered over at me, noticing my elevated breathing rate and soft moaning.

"Are you enjoying your lamb, Jade?" he said.

"Oh yes," I sighed, trying to keep my composure while his daughter foot-fucked me under the table. "It's quite...*succulent*."

"Shakriya is one of our most popular dishes in Turkey," he nodded. "But the chefs here seem to have a special knack for bringing out its unique flavors. I'll have to ask them what their secret ingredient is."

"Yes," I moaned. "They seem quite skilled. I haven't enjoyed a meal quite this stimulating in a long time."

As he and Adele continued chatting about their growing banking partnership, I dared not even *look* at Leila for fear of betraying what she was doing to me under the table. Just when I thought it couldn't possibly get any more awkward and titillating, she suddenly thrust her big toe inside my pussy, curling the rest of her foot against my burning clit. I gasped in surprise, and Omar peered over at me in alarm.

"Are you alright, Jade?" he said. "Are you choking on something?"

"No," I said, bringing my napkin to my mouth to distract attention from my rapidly escalating arousal. "A piece of lamb just went down the wrong way. I'll have to slow down a bit while I'm eating. I think I'm just getting a little carried away with this sumptuous dish."

"It's definitely meant to be savored," he said, smiling at me politely. "But watch out for those spices. There's quite a bit of garlic and paprika in there. It'll burn your mouth if you're not careful."

"Yes," I panted. "I can feel it burning already."

"How about *you*, dear?" Omar said, turning to look at his unusually quiet daughter. "Are you enjoying your meal equally as much?"

"Yes father," Leila said. "I'm just enjoying listening in on your conversation with Adele. I find the world of finance fascinating."

"I'm glad you find it interesting," he said. "I'm looking

forward to placing you in an important position in my business when you graduate from Harvard."

"Yes father," Leila nodded obediently while flexing her toes inside my dripping cunt.

As Omar and Adele continued their conversation, Leila quietly picked away at her dish with her knife and fork clinking against the fine china while she pretended to be absorbed in their discussion. Before long, the combination of her deft toe-fucking and tickling of my clit with the rest of her foot brought me to the brink of climax, and I fought valiantly to maintain my composure as my orgasm quickly swept over me. Trying to remain still in my chair, I couldn't help expressing the joy in my face as a deep rash suddenly poured over my cheeks and my eyes began to water from the intense pleasure emanating within my body.

Noticing my discomfort once again, Omar turned toward me with a concerned expression.

"Too much garlic?" he said, offering me a glass of water.

"Too much *something*," I said, gulping down the water trying to keep his attention focused above the table. "But it's very stimulating. I think I just need to acclimate more to your customs and cuisine. I'm looking forward to enjoying more of these delicacies once I land in your country."

"I'm looking forward to sharing more of our culture with *both* of you as my guests," he nodded, turning toward his daughter. "Don't you agree, Leila? We'll have to show these women some proper Turkish hospitality."

"Absolutely father," Leila said, beaming at both Adele and me. "There's so much more I'd love to show these lovely ladies."

For the rest of the meal, the four of us talked about our past experiences and future plans, while Omar and Leila raved about the various attractions awaiting us in their home town. I was looking forward to exploring the ancient city of Istanbul, but I was much *more* interested in exploring what other secrets Leila might be hiding. If her expert massage of my private areas was any indication, I expected her to be quite a minx when she was freed from her father's oversight. But I also knew it would be difficult for me to wait the remaining four days for our train to reach its final destination before I could have more of her. While Omar graciously offered to pay for our meal and thanked the waiter for his excellent service, I quietly slipped a note under Leila's napkin with my room number.

With any luck, she'd be able to find some time to slip away later in the evening to join me in my private boudoir.

4

———

After dinner, the four of us returned to our individual staterooms to catch up on email and change out of our formal wear. By now, the train had reached the Swiss border, and I looked out the window peering up the soaring Alps. The juxtaposition of the lush green valleys and the snow-covered mountains provided a calming culmination to my exciting first day on the Orient Express, and I soon fell asleep from the soft rumbling of the train as it sliced its way through the deep canyons.

I awoke a few hours later to a soft tap on my door, and I threw on the plush terrycloth robe hanging in the bathroom while I approached the cabin door warily. In my still-groggy stupor, I'd temporarily forgotten about the note I left for Leila in the dining car, but when I saw her through the peephole, my pussy throbbed in excitement. I opened the door and noticed that she'd changed into skinny jeans and a tight t-shirt that hugged every inch of her curvy body.

"Leila," I said, peering into the hall to make sure she was alone. "I wasn't sure if you got my message..."

"I had to wait a few hours for my father to settle into his stateroom." she said. "I think maybe he has a visitor, so I've got a little time while he's distracted–"

"Come in," I said, practically yanking her out of the hallway into my bedroom. "*God*, you look so sexy. I haven't been able to stop thinking about you all day."

Without saying a word, Leila placed her thumbs under the bottom of my belt and pulled it apart, dropping my robe to the floor. For a moment, I stood stark naked in front of her, shocked at the boldness of her action for someone her age.

"Something tells me this isn't the first time you've done something like this," I panted, feeling my nipples hardening as she admired my yoga-studio-toned body.

"It's the first time I've done this with a *woman*," she said, running her hands softly around the sides of my heaving breasts.

"Not counting earlier today," I smiled.

"Right, but that hardly counts. It was far too quick and one-sided. I've been wanting to fuck you ever since I watched you touching yourself in the bar car."

"Let's get you out of those clothes," I said, pulling her toward the bed. "This time I want to touch *every* part of your magnificent body."

The two of us flopped down on top of the mattress while we unbuttoned and tugged off her clothes, until she lay nude beside me. We pulled each other close and intertwined our legs as we pressed our breasts together, kissing passionately.

"*Damn*, girl," I panted. "You sure don't act like a schoolgirl."

"No?" she said, gazing at me coyly. "How exactly are schoolgirls my age *supposed* to act?"

"Like *this*," I said, flipping her onto her back and leaning over her while I grabbed her firm tits in my palms and suckled her erect teats like a hungry calf.

"No fair," she panted, arching her back as I threaded my thigh between her legs toward her steaming pussy. "It's my turn to lick *you* this time."

"You'll have your chance soon enough," I said, placing my palm over her crotch and plunging two fingers inside her wet tunnel. "Right now, I just want to *look* at you while I caress you all over."

As I finger-fucked her with my hand, she squirmed on the bed and peered up at me with parted lips.

"Do you *like* that?" I taunted her. "Do you like being probed while you lie pinned on the mattress, only able to peer back at me?"

"You mean the same way I fucked you with my foot under the table in the restaurant?" she smirked.

"Exactly," I said. "That was very rude of you. You put me in an uncomfortable position sitting right next to your father."

"You didn't seem to mind it too much at the time. Besides, he seemed preoccupied with your lady friend. He had no clue what I was doing to you under the table."

"You're a very naughty girl," I said, pushing her over onto her side while I spread her legs into a scissor position. "Now it's my turn to have my way with *you*. I'm going to fuck your sweet pussy and watch you whimper and moan the same way you did with me."

I raised myself up into a kneeling position and straddled her thighs, pushing my pussy toward hers, then I tilted my hips until our vulvas merged, rocking my wet lips against hers. Leila groaned softly, reaching up to squeeze my tits, but I extended her upper leg and swung it between my breasts, pulling her harder against me.

"*Fuck* yes," Leila hissed, throwing her head back against the mattress. "Fuck my cunt with your wet pussy, Jade. That feels so good."

"Better than my *head* between your legs?" I smiled, humping her more vigorously.

"Yes," she grunted. "At least this time I can *see* what you're doing to me."

"That works *both* ways, young lady. I far prefer looking at your pretty face than having your tartan skirt pulled over my head."

"Oh?" she smirked. "You didn't enjoy eating out the innocent schoolgirl in the private lavatory?"

"Not as much as I did sucking on my lambchops while you fucked me with your foot under the table in full view of all the other restaurant patrons."

"You seem to have a predilection for dangerous public sex," she smiled.

"Maybe," I said. "But I also like having you all to myself, where I can live out *all* my fantasies in the privacy of my own bedroom."

"You better hurry up then," Leila panted, digging her nails into the side of my hips as our pussies slurped loudly over the background rumble of the train. "Before my father looks in on me and sees that I've disappeared from my cabin."

"Yes, baby," I groaned. "I'm going to cum all over your sweet pussy while I imagine all the dirty things I want to do to you. Come with me while I grind my cunt against yours."

"Yes, Jade," Leila panted. "I'm close. Fuck me harder. Let me feel your tits caressing my leg while I gush all over your twat."

"Holy *fuck*," I screamed, suddenly overcome with passion at her dirty talk and the look of pleasure on her face as her mouth widened approaching her climax. Suddenly, her body jerked violently, and I felt a gush of fluid spraying all over the inside of my thighs as a crimson flush spread over her upper chest and face.

"Oh God, Leila," I hissed. "I'm cumming baby. I'm cumming all over your sweet, slippery pussy."

While I wrapped both of my arms around her leg, now pointing straight up in the air between my bouncing tits, I felt my pussy clamp down hard as I emitted hard jets of my own all over her pulsing hole. Between the two of us, our juices were spraying in every direction, and I blinked as it squirted all the way up into my eyes. But I hardly cared, reveling in the sensation of our commingled love juices running down over the front of my face while she stared up at me.

After we both finished coming hard, I collapsed onto the bed beside Leila and we giggled as we spread our lubrication all over our breasts and stomachs.

"That was *insane*!" Leila panted, rolling over to kiss me. "Who knew having sex with a *woman* could be so much fun?"

"And *sticky*!" I said, rolling her nipples softly between my slippery fingers.

"I thought *I* was the only one who squirted like that," she said.

"So did I," I smiled. "You're the first one I've been with who could do it with me at the same time."

"What other firsts can you teach me before my daddy catches me breaking curfew?" Leila asked.

"Well," I said, reaching into my nightstand for the

double-sided dildo I'd packed hoping for a moment precisely like this. "Have you ever tried one of *these*?"

"Not one as long and flexible as that one," she said, peering up at the silicone dildo as I shook it in the air. "Is that what I *think* it is?"

"That depends what you think it is," I smiled. "You can use this thing in so many interesting ways."

"*Show* me," Leila purred. "I think it's about time one of us got fucked with something bigger than a finger or a toe."

"I thought you'd never ask," I said. "Assume the position."

"Which position did you have in mind?" she grinned. "I mean, it looks like you could fuck me with that thing in all manner of positions."

"That's true," I nodded. "I've tried it with both of us on our backs, on our knees ass-to-ass, and even in the pile-driver position. But this time, I want to be close to you while we enjoy it together. Let's sit facing each other on the bed while we kiss and hold hands. It might be fun to watch each other while we're both humping this thing."

"You seem to have a lot of experience trying different things with women," Leila said.

"It wasn't always this way," I said. "But once you decide to go *femme*, you quickly learn there's no longer any need for men."

"Ha, ha," Leila chuckled. "Especially when we have our choice of giant phalluses. I'm in—fill me up with that thing. This time I'm going to watch you squirt all over my pussy while we come together."

"You're way ahead of me, girl," I smiled, positioning my hips in front of hers and spreading my knees apart as I inserted one end of the long dildo into Leila's box before pressing my hips forward and thrusting the other end in my hole while we clasped hands and moaned feeling the instrument filling us both up.

"Uhnn," Leila groaned, watching the pink appendage disappear into our slits as we began to rock our hips together, gazing excitedly into each other's eyes. It didn't take long for the sight and sensation of the double-sided dildo plowing in and out of our flapping pussies to have the desired effect, and within minutes we were both moaning and squirming on the bed, squeezing our hands tightly together as both of our mouths parted and we stared into each other's eyes nearing another mutual climax. When we both tipped over the edge, our eyes darted down between our legs, where we watched with joyful celebration as our pussies squirted powerful streams of lubrication over each other's stomachs.

It seemed to take forever for the two of us to stop cumming, but when our orgasms finally began to subside, we flopped down on the bed in opposite directions, peering outside the picture window at the snow-capped mountains passing by.

"Talk about a *peak experience*," Leila panted.

"You got *that* right, girl," I moaned contentedly.

Suddenly, we heard a loud tap on the cabin door and we both jerked upright, looking at each other with frightened eyes.

"You don't think that's–" Leila shuddered.

"Let's hope not," I said, thinking the same thing. "Why don't you lock yourself in the washroom just in case, while I check out who it is. Don't worry, if it's your father, I'll tell him I haven't seen you since dinner."

"Thanks," Leila said, scurrying into the washroom and closing the door behind her.

I straightened my hair, then pulled on my robe and

approached the door cautiously. When I looked out the peephole, I was relieved to see Adele peering back at me. I opened the door a crack, not wanting her to invade Leila's privacy, and placed my face against the opening.

"Adele!" I said, pretending to be surprised. "What brings you back this way so late at night?"

"I was hoping you might be interested in picking up where we left off earlier in the day," she said. "I've been thinking about you ever since we shared that intimate moment together in the bar car."

"I've been thinking the same thing," I said. "But it's getting late and I'm kind of tired–"

"Who are you kidding?" she said, forcing my door open. "This room *reeks* of sex. Something tells me you haven't been alone in here all this time..."

"I don't know what you mean–" I protested, trying to block her ingress.

She took one look at my messy bed and smiled back at me.

"Just as I thought," she smiled. "You obviously haven't been alone. And by the look of that glistening sex toy on the bed, I suspect you've been mixing it up with that cute Arab girl once again."

"That wouldn't be appropriate..."

"Oh *please*," Adele huffed, barging past me. "Where *is* she? You didn't think I knew what you two were up to over dinner below her father's line of sight?"

"I don't know what you're talking about–"

"With all your moaning and fawning over your spicy curry? Remember, I was sitting right next to you. You practically gave me a charley horse knocking your legs against mine while Leila foot-fucked you under the table."

"Was it that obvious?" I said, resigning myself to the obvious.

"Only to *me*, apparently. Her father was too busy gaping at my tight bosom and trying to negotiate more favorable banking terms to realize what the two of you were doing right under his nose."

"Thanks for that," I sighed. "But I'm not sure Leila's quite ready to bring another partner into the picture just yet..."

Suddenly, the bathroom door parted open and Leila stuck her head out, peering at us with wide eyes.

"I *knew* it!" Adele said. "The *least* you guys can do is share in the spoils, since I've been the one keeping her dad occupied while the two of you were getting your groove on in here."

"So it was *you* who was in the room with him this evening," Leila said, stepping out from behind the door completely naked.

"I saw Jade passing the note to you over dinner and figured the two of you would be looking for some more quiet time together," Adele nodded. "I just hoped to get in on the fun while your father thinks you're still resting in your cabin."

"What do you say, Leila?" I said, peering at her with a coy smile. "Do you think you've got enough time for a little more girl-on-girl action?"

Leila paused for a moment appraising Adele's sexy body, still clad in her clingy lace dress.

"The more the merrier," she smiled. "Now that I've got a taste for women, I want to sample *all* the offerings before this trip is over."

"Come try a little *French* cuisine then," Adele said, clasping Leila's hand and leading her over to the ruffled bed.

I stuck my head outside the door to make sure no one else was spying, then I closed it softly behind me.

This luxury train ride was turning out to have a lot more extra amenities than I could have wished for. As I plopped down on the bed next to the two women, we all intertwined our legs and moaned as we began caressing and disrobing our new partner-in-crime.

VICTORIA RUSH

Everybody's an exhibitionist in disguise

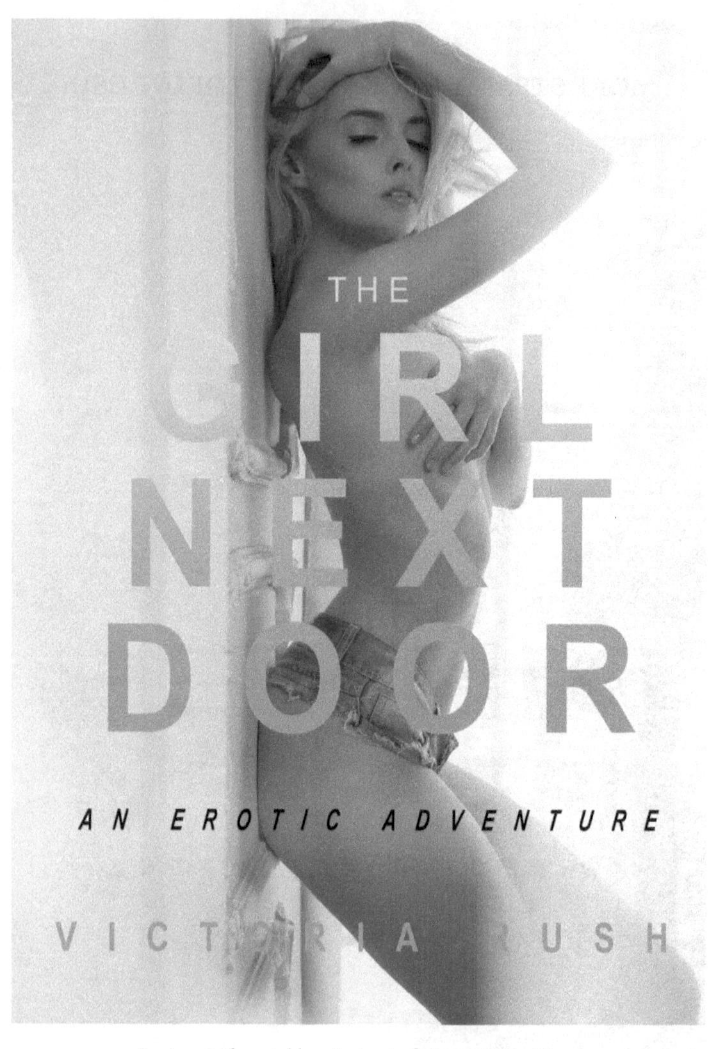

Spying on the neighbors just got a lot more interesting...

Everything's sexier in the dark...

NUDE CRUISE

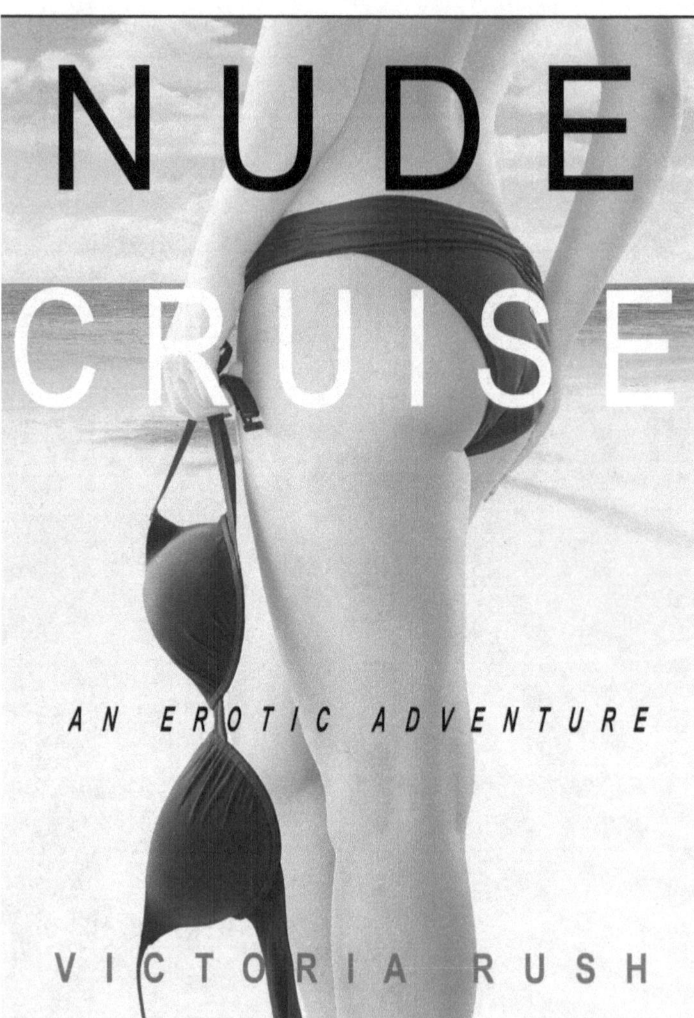

AN EROTIC ADVENTURE

VICTORIA RUSH

Some people get wet on a cruise for different reasons...

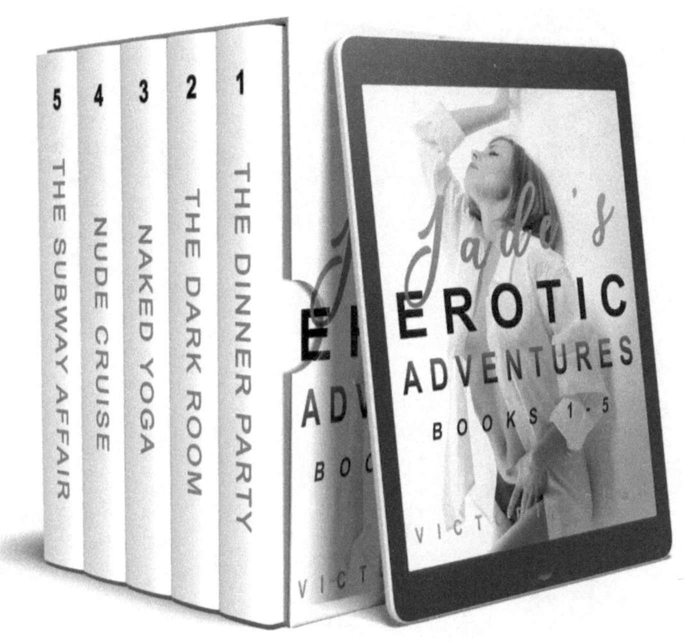

Books 1 -5 in the bestselling erotica series - 60% off

THE DARE - PREVIEW
CHAPTER 3

"Okay, so now that I'm committed, tell me where you had in mind for this little experiment."

"Actually," Hannah said, "I have a *series* of places in mind, each one more challenging than the one before."

"But I thought you said this was a one-off proposition?"

"I said nothing of the sort. I only said that if you won, I'd pay for the flights to Bora Bora. If you want me to cover the cost of hotels, food, and all the other incidentals, you'll have to pass progressively tougher tests. We don't want to make this *too* easy for you, do we?"

I crossed my arms and huffed, putting on my best pouty face.

"It hardly seems fair," I said. "But I'm still game. Besides, either one of us can pull out at any time to lock in our gains, right?"

"I suppose so," Hannah shrugged. "But what would be the fun in that? Something tells me once you've tried the first experiment, you won't want to stop. I think you're going to find this whole thing quite titillating and exciting. This will be the most fun either one of us has had in a long time."

I pushed the rest of my half-eaten salmon dish to the side, suddenly no longer interested in eating.

"Okay, lay it on me then. Where are you planning to take me for the first test?

Hannah gulped down the rest of her margarita then peered at me with a lopsided grin.

"Church. More specifically, a *Catholic* church. You haven't been in quite a while, have you? This will be your chance to repent and atone for all your sins."

"It's not like I've broken any commandments or anything–"

"The Catholic Church still considers sex outside of marriage a mortal sin. So technically, you've been doing a ton of sinning since your marriage ended."

"Well I haven't been a practicing Catholic for ages," I snorted. "So my conscience is clear. This'll be a cakewalk. All I have to do is sit quietly in my pew, right?"

"Yes, but it'll be a *front-row* pew, in full view of the priest who'll be delivering the sermon."

"Okay, but I'll be fully clothed, right? It's not like there'll be anything for him to see..."

"Not if you can keep your composure and don't cum all over the floor," Hannah said, cocking her head playfully.

"I don't think I'll have any difficulty keeping my dick in my pants, in a manner of speaking. But you raise a good point. You can't expect me not to get a little wet while you're stimulating me. What will I be allowed to wear?"

"I assume you'll dress appropriately, wearing your Sunday best. A mid-length skirt and button-up blouse should do the trick. You should be able to hide a few dribbles that way, right?"

"I suppose so, but how will we muffle the sound of the vibrator buzzing inside my panties? There's likely to be other people sitting around me in adjacent pews..."

"Never fear," Hannah smiled, reaching into her purse and pulling out a U-shaped silicone sex toy. "I've been talking with our friend at the local Babeland store. She's given me the latest prototype of the We-Vibe vibrator to test." She held up a smaller device with two control buttons and a flywheel. "Complete with a Bluetooth remote control. And the best thing is that it's whisper-quiet.

"Here," she said, handing me the flexible device. "See for yourself."

She tapped one of the buttons on the remote and the thick side of the contraption began buzzing softly in my hand.

"Okay," I nodded, looking around me to see if any other restaurant patrons were distracted by the gentle hum of the object. "It's *quiet* enough, but which end goes inside?"

"The bulbous end is a natural G-spot stimulator. You place the flatter end against your clit, then pull the thing up tight against your vulva to keep it snugly in place."

I suddenly became mindful of the wetness permeating my panties as I imagined the device vibrating inside me, surrounded by a bunch of oblivious bystanders.

"Can I give it a try here, like we did last time?" I grinned.

"No way," Hannah said, pulling the toy out of my hands. "There'll be no trial runs for this or any future tests. You'll just have to wait until we get to the church."

"And where will *you* be sitting while this is all going down?" I said.

"Right next to you, of course. I'll want a front-row seat to watch all the action."

———

On Sunday morning, Hannah picked me up and drove me the two miles to our local church. The entire time I squirmed in my seat trying to imagine what it would be like having a vibrator buzzing inside me in the quiet chapel. When we got to the church parking lot, she pulled into a sheltered space then plucked the blue vibrator out of her purse and handed it to me, resting her arm on the seat cushion expectantly.

"*What?*" I said. "You don't trust me to put it in privately?"

"Not really," she smirked. "For all I know, you might pull on some adult diapers under your skirt to hide any unintended releases. Here," she said, handing me a plastic vial. "I brought some lube to make it go in easier."

"I don't need any," I said, pulling the vibrator out of her hands and placing it under my skirt. "I'm already plenty worked up thinking about this scenario."

"I hope you're wearing panties under that skirt," Hannah said, watching me shift my weight as I placed the device against my vulva. "We wouldn't want it popping out at an inopportune moment."

"I'll just have to leave that up to your imagination," I sneered, lifting my skirt halfway up my thigh. "Unless you need to inspect the goods to make sure I'm not cheating."

"I trust you," Hannah smiled, opening her car door. "Something tells me you're looking forward to this just as much as I am."

As we approached the entrance to the church, I noticed a familiar figure standing at the top of the steps greeting the incoming parishioners, and he made eye contact with me when Hannah and I approached the landing.

"Jade!" Father Fife said, holding out his hands to me. "I haven't seen you in such a long time. It's so good to have you join us again."

"I'm sorry, Father," I said, placing my sweaty hand between his. "I've been a little distracted lately..."

"Life has a habit of getting in the way of the important things," he said. "We're just glad to have you whenever you can find time." He turned to Hannah, raising his eyebrows in curiosity. "And who's this lovely lady you've brought with you to attend our service today?"

"This is Hannah," I said, motioning toward my friend. "I thought I'd bring her along for moral support."

"Happy to have you, Hannah," Father Fife said, clasping Hannah's hands warmly. "The Lord knows we all need moral support wherever we can find it."

Hannah nodded politely, then the two of us walked through the entrance doors where I dipped my hand into the bowl of holy water and crossed my chest before continuing on toward the front of the chapel.

"*Jesus*," Hannah whispered, peering around the imposing shrine. "Is it just me, or did that feel a little creepy? All that talk about *having* us and that prolonged hand-holding. Hasn't he been paying any attention to the me-too movement?"

"I'm not sure any of that applies to men of the *cloth*," I chuckled. "But you better be careful about using the Lord's name like that around here. If anybody overhears you, you're liable to be burned at the stake."

The two of us stepped lively down the main aisle and finding a free spot in the front row, we took our seats flanked by two elderly couples. It was hard to imagine how Hannah would be able to use the remote-control device sandwiched so closely between other parishioners, and I crossed my legs, thankful for the brief respite. When everyone had filed into the chapel and the bell signaled the start of the service, a hush fell over the chamber and we all stood up as Father Fife walked onto the pulpit in his flowing robes.

"In the name of the Father, and of the Son, and of the Holy Spirit," he intoned solemnly.

"Amen," the congregation murmured in unison.

"The Lord be with you," he said.

"And with your spirit," the couples beside me retorted.

What the hell have I gotten myself into? I thought, feeling the flexible vibrator pressing against the inside of my closed legs. I didn't consider myself a terribly religious person, but being in this holy place surrounded by all the familiar rituals brought back all the old memories from my parents about the consequences of sinful behavior. *Surely getting secretly stimulated by a sex toy in the house of God will send me straight to hell.*

This was the point in the church service where everybody was supposed to take a moment to make a penitential act. While I listened to the other parishioners around me making their supplications, my knees began shaking as I made my own silent prayer for forgiveness.

"May Almighty God have mercy on us all," the priest said. "Forgive us our sins, and bring us to everlasting life."

"Amen," I joined in the congregation's response.

"Let us pray," Father Fife said, bowing his head.

As we closed our eyes and he began his opening prayer, Hannah nudged me with her knee and my mind raced with images of the pastor scornfully looking down at us while we played our blasphemous game. I peered up as he flapped his Bible closed, and caught him glancing in my direction.

"Through our Lord Jesus Christ, your Son," he said. "Who lives and reigns with you in the unity of the Holy Spirit, one God forever and ever."

"Amen," I said aloud, hoping he'd see me behaving like a good Catholic girl and turn his attention elsewhere.

He motioned for everyone to sit down and I was glad to get off my shaky feet onto the relative safety of the wooden pew.

"Good morning, ladies and gentlemen," he began his homily. "Today, I would like to talk with you about *morality*. Specifically, about the decaying state of society's morals in today's world. All around us we are surrounded by prurient symbols of modern decadence. First it was in the form of the printed word, then motion pictures, then the ubiquitous internet. It seems everywhere we turn, we are bombarded with profane and sacrilegious images."

I felt my heart pounding in my chest, like he was singling me out personally for my not-so-infrequent porn surfing.

"We seem to have forgotten," he railed, "the Lord's commandment that we shall not covet thy neighbor's wife. This admonition can be taken in its broadest context. Not only have many of you forsaken the sacred institution of marriage, but the egregious and widespread popularity of obscene *pornography* belies our unbridled lust and depravity. God slew Onan for spilling his seed, and so He will strike all others who practice self-abuse."

Hannah nudged her knee against mine, suddenly

reminding me why we were here. I was glad that she hadn't yet had the opportunity to take out her remote-control device, and I prayed that we'd be able to get through most of the service without her rudely interrupting it. I'd already begun to regret agreeing to this little venture, and I hoped that somehow we'd be able to bypass this first phase in her experiment.

"I'd like you to pick up your Bibles," Father Fife said, interrupting my thoughts. "And turn to Mark, Chapter 7, Verse 20."

Hannah and I reached down to pick up the bibles lying on the seat beside each of us, and we flipped to the indicated section.

"Read this passage with me, my friends," Father Fife instructed. "What comes *out* of a person is what defiles him," he enunciated, while the congregation quietly murmured along.

As I began to recite the passage along with him, I saw Hannah reach into her side pocket and place her closed hand between the book binding.

"For from within come evil thoughts," I continued reading as I peered out of the corner of my eye to see what she was up to.

"Sexual immorality, adultery, coveting, wickedness..." we read in unison.

Suddenly, I felt the interior end of the vibrator begin to tremble inside me and I stuttered, trying to finish the passage.

"Deceit...sensuality...envy..." I stammered, trying to catch my breath as I followed along. Hearing my labored recital, Hannah turned her head in my direction, acknowledging my silent suffering. She knew exactly what I was feeling and how difficult it was for me to remain composed as I read the script.

"All these evil things...come from *within*," I gulped as I began to feel the pleasure spread across my pelvic region. "And they defile a person."

"Consider these words carefully," the priest said, surveying my hunched-over posture. "For the Lord does not abide salacious thoughts and behavior. If you want passage into His Kingdom, you must be as pure and righteous as He."

He paused for a moment to let the message sink in, then he motioned with his two hands for us to be seated. I was grateful for the rest, and I froze upright in my chair trying to ignore the movement of the possessed instrument inside me.

"Let us consider for a moment *another* one of God's ten commandments," Father Fife continued. "Thou shall not commit *adultery*. The Lord made Eve from the flesh of Adam, and in so doing signified that forever more man shall be united to his wife as one..."

As Father Fife ramped up the intensity of his gayphobic critique, so did Hannah, furtively adjusting the flywheel on the remote-control device nestled under her palm in her lap. As she slowly increased the speed of the vibrations emanating inside my pussy, I squirmed on the bench, trying to restrain my rising passion.

"By rejecting the sanctity of marriage," Father Fife continued, glancing distractedly in my direction, "you have all *sinned*. In the book of Deuteronomy, we saw that God ordered adulterers be stoned to death. For your indiscriminate behavior, so shall the Lord indiscriminately smite thee."

Jesus, I thought. If that's what awaits a sinner for

cheating on their spouse, I wonder what happens to someone who self-abuses herself while sitting for Sunday Service in a house of God. *Surely I'll burn in hell for this act of sacrilege.*

Just when I thought I was beginning to get control over the delicious sensations stimulating my insides, Father Fife instructed us to stand once again and recite another passage from the Bible.

"Please stand now and read Peter 1:16 with me," he said.

Everyone stood and dutifully flipped to the relevant section of the scriptures. This time it was even harder for me to stand motionless, as my knees fluttered unsteadily from the pleasurable sensations radiating inside me.

"It is written..." I tried to read along. "That you shall be holy, for I am holy."

I saw Hannah's hands moving once again inside her prayer book, and suddenly I felt the *other* end of the U-shaped vibrator buzzing against my clit.

"And now Galatians 5:16," Father Fife instructed, barely giving me a chance to recover.

I flipped to the new citation and gasped for breath as my legs wobbled beneath me.

"But I say," I panted unsteadily. "Walk by the Spirit, and you will not gratify the desires of the flesh."

"So it is written," Father Fife said, closing his Bible. "Be righteous as the Lord, and you shall join him in Heaven for everlasting days. And now," he said, magnifying my torture. "I would like us to sing together one of my favorite hymns celebrating His blessing, *Amazing Grace*. Please pick up your hymn books and turn to page forty-three."

"Amazing grace, how sweet the sound," the priest began to sing as the entire congregation joined him in harmony.

"That saved a wretch like me," I sang along, trying to

ignore the message that seemed targeted directly at me. As I tried to hold the melody, Hannah cupped the remote-control device in her hand and turned the flywheel to its maximum setting.

"I once was lost, but now am found," I hyperventilated, pressing my legs together as hard as I could to stifle the rising passion that threatened to overtake me.

"Was blind, but now I see," I squealed, singing the last word decidedly off-pitch as Father Fife turned to see my entire body shaking as I belted the famous hymn.

By the time I'd finished the song, I'd somehow managed to keep it together and fight off the cresting passion that had threatened to put me over the edge. When we finally sat back down, Hannah mercifully turned the vibrator off, and I spread my hands over my ruffled skirt to signal that I'd managed to keep myself composed.

When the service was over and we walked up the aisle behind the rest of the assembly to exit the church, I couldn't wait to get out of the building to wash myself off, figuratively and literally. I was glad that we were at the back of the crowd so nobody could see the back of my skirt. I wasn't sure if my leaking pussy had left a stain, but I sure as hell didn't want one of the parishioners pointing it out. When we finally exited the entrance doors, Father Fife turned to the two of us and smiled.

"I noticed you seemed a little more passionate than usual reciting today's passages, Jade" he said to me.

"Yes, Father," I said, shaking his hand unsteadily. "I felt truly embodied by the spirit."

"And *you*, Hannah," he nodded. "Did you enjoy today's service also?"

"Oh yes," she said. "It was the most moving sermon I've attended in a long time."

"I hope you'll both come again," Father Fife said to the two of us.

"I'm sure we *will*, Father," Hannah smiled as we continued down the steps.

Like the second we get back home, I thought to myself, dying to tear off my clothes and squirt all over Hannah's face while she ate out my still-dripping pussy.

READ MORE...

ABOUT THE AUTHOR

If you would like to receive notification of new book(s) in Jade's Erotic Adventures, follow me at http://bookbub.com/authors/victoria-rush.

If you have a moment, please post a brief review on my Amazon book page at viewbook.at/orientexpress . Even just a couple of sentences will help other readers find and enjoy this book as much as you hopefully did.

Follow, share, like, and comment at:

www.facebook.com/authorvictoriarush
www.pinterest.com/authorvictoriarush
www.twitter.com/authorvictoriarush
authorvictoriarush@outlook.com

Hope to see you again soon!